The Computer Is Down

Evangelina Vigil-Piñón

Arte Publico Press

Houston

Acknowledgements

The following poems first appeared in these publications: "telephone line," "dumb broad!" and "the bridge people" in *Woman of Her Word: Hispanic Women Write* (Arte Publico Press, 1983); "time bomb" and "one quiet moment" in *Third Woman*, 3/1–2 (1986); "death has been hard to bear" (retitled, "city cemetery") in *Houston Poetry Fest Anthology, 1986* (Images, INK, 1986).

This book is made possible through a grant from the National Endowment for the Arts, a federal agency.

Arte Público Press
University of Houston
Houston, Texas 77004

ISBN 0-934770-32-8
LC 83072576

Printed in the United States of America

he
Computer
Is Down
vangelina
igil-
iñón
ARTE
PUBLICO
PRESS

Table of Contents

For Marc Antony

space city

to the architects of the future

it is imperative
that you own a spacecraft
to glide you through the flightways
glistening spaceships
of metallic colors
others, in flight
destiny in their hearts
and in their minds
the mystery of time:
but, don't
don't look back
you disrupt your concentration
for, you *are* a pilot
mind the journey,
the glamour,
the greatness!

approaching Interstate 45!
exciting rollercoaster ride
encircling citylights
starlights
dark monolithic structures
glittering in geometrics

exiting IH 10!
zipping down the curving lanes
reflecting a crimson sunset
a wash of pastel skies
mirrored in your eyes
the legacy of generations
maybe one day
to crumble down with history
or, maybe to stand in triumph
along with *all* else
that will have outlived
the eons and eons of immeasureable time

which make up
infinity

so, native
traveler,
extra-terrestrial!
slip on your shades!
fasten the seatbelt!
adjust the space helmet!
enjoy this one-way glide
through time
speeding to
the future!

transference

i.

with a dashing smile
a handsome Black busdriver welcomes you on board
you and the Salvadorean lady that you met at the stop
she had hurriedly splashed Oil of Olay on her face
suddenly, self-conscious, uttering
"Ay, disculpe, señorita. Es que . . ."
proceeding to explain that in this country
people are always in a hurry
even when there's no need!
she exclaimed,
tightening the cap on the bottle

you take a seat by the window
as the bus advances to the next stop
where, on hops
a young Puerto Rican
sporting a white starched shirt and tie
overcoat, umbrella and lunchbag in hand
he walks down the aisle
smiling flirtatiously at the ladies
and nodding a courtly good morning
to an old white gent
seated towards the rear of the bus
who must remember this old neighborhood
in those thriving years
quaint post-war redbrick houses
neatly-trimmed patches of green
shade trees abounding
a legacy of hard times
and hard work
inspired by the American Dream
now transformed
to meet the future
on equal grounds

and the bus advances
the heads of passengers bopping
their postures swaying to the motion of the bus

as it glides over bumps and dips
their eyes gazing through dark glass windows
STOP
says the sign
in red and white
the bus stops, perpendicular to the freeway
where traffic rolls at the erratic pace of 8 o'clockers
running late
some didn't find the time to pack a lunch
another junk food excursion expected at noon, no doubt
a preoccupation that must be dismissed
the traffic demands it
metallic bodies
glistening in the eastern sunlight
meandering down curving lanes
brake lights flashing
on and off
in sequential delay
"Put your blinker on, dumbass!"
some are surely thinking
while others might be conjuring their tardy excuses
as they race with time
"What time does that read?
Sixty-four degrees.
Darn, I missed it!"
some surely are fretting over their forgetfulness
as the radio weatherman issues the forecast
a few, likely, are prepared
"Sure am glad I wore my space helmet—
looks like acid rain in the horizon."

the bus proceeds alongside the freeway
bound toward the concrete skyline
at the threshold of downtown
billboards captivate the eye with every glance
a montage of seductresses
"Es tan suave"
beckons the sophisticated lady
in black satin
her moist, red lips enticing you
to taste that whiskey *importado*
adjacent, a glamorous model poses

her elegant fingers balancing a cigarette
filtering smoke
her ebony face is frozen in a smile
of lasting satisfaction

the next stop is Viet-Town
its landmark, an oversized rectangular sign
stark, one-dimensional red letters
on a bright flat yellow background
V I E T N A M   P L A Z A
around here, not many wait on buses
they walk it
or ride bikes
or some cruise in their Mercedes Benz's
but the derelicts
they love to ride the bus
gives them somewhere to go
"Oh, no," a passenger cringes
in reluctant anticipation
as a bum climbs on board
his stench instantly mingling
with the fragrances of Polo
Estēe Lauder
and Oil of Olay
"What a relief!"
the passenger sighs
as the bum mumbles something to the driver
and is let off at the next stop
where on hops another
grumbling to himself
and everybody holds their breath
as he staggers to the rear
holding on to the support railing

and the bus advances
cutting through dark morning shadows
cast by pastel skyscrapers
the hues of sand, sea and skies
"Gimme a transfer"
the decrepit skid utters to the driver
"Ah don' wn' go ov' th' bridge."
and the driver tears the slip

and hands it to him
and one common act
alters the course of a half-man's destiny
the price, a free strip of recycled paper
bearing meaningless schedules, transfer points
and destinations
one wretched soul's documentation
of transference

ii.

click-click clock-clock
high heels conquering concrete
sidewalks with their familiar cracks
and unpredictable dips

from the parking lot you approach the order of the day
from the corner of one eye you discern
silhouettes emerging from the banks of the bayou
you step up your pace,
catching up with a woman in a business suit
"Pretty bad, huh?"
"'Morning" she responds
and the urgency of the 8 o'clock hour
averts further contemplation
a man walks hurriedly ahead of you
his hand clutching tightly
a leather briefcase
at the doors of the courthouse
you catch up with him
"Morning" you nod
his face remains expressionless
as he enters before you

as the elevator ascends
your thoughts descend
to the banks of the bayou
you marvel at the adaptive abilities of these human creatures
but suddenly, with a start
further thought is dismissed
why ponder the grotesque aspects of the greater metropolis?
much more pleasureable

savoring a cup of coffee
gazing out an ninth floor window
viewing the vastness of the heavens
an immensity of blue
holding one's perceptions of aesthetics
intact:

the earth in timely motion
the sun illuminating man's creations
futuristic structures lending eyeful form
at once, concrete and abstract
testimony to the capacity of the human mind
that can imagine
beyond
a horizon

the system

i.

it is imperative that you verify the balance
punch the seven digits
the first ring is interrupted by a Click!
the background is static
to the anticipated recorded voice
You have reached MBank.
All lines are busy.
Your call has been automatically placed on hold.
Please continue to hold,
and the next available teller will assist you.
Please do not hang up,
as this may delay the servicing of your call.
Thank you for calling MBank.
Click!
and on comes the beautiful muzak
programmed to appease impatience
in one ear, the lackadaisical medley of nameable tunes
in the other, a steady stream of audible demands on the job:
incoming calls that buzz on
like panic buttons
in synchronous reaction
"Line one is for you."
"A Mr. Smith on line three wants to hold for you."
surely the next available teller will assist you soon
but the relaxed ear hears only promises of nostalgic dreams
while telephone lines on hold
blink on and off
off and on
with urgency

abruptly, the golden voice of yesteryear is interrupted
by a voice, impersonally polite
"MBank, may I help you?"
"Yes, please. I'd like to check on my account ba—"
"I'm sorry, . . ."
"lance."
". . . but the computer is down.

Please call back later."
"Thanks"
you say
to a dial tone.

ii.

somehow you must break through
that monstrous network
of public confidential information
punch the digits
busy
punch the digits
still busy!
punch the digits
(no wonder Orwell knew their number)
it's ringing!
no . . . wait—Click!
and the familiar static of the hold button
registers on
a high-pitched voice enunciates
slowly and with deliberateness
You have reached the offices of the Internal Revenue Service.
Please have your Social Security or
Identification Number ready.
Do not hung up, as this may—
but you do
opting for the delay
and the interest.

iii.

touch the seven numbered tones
the line is busy
somehow you knew this before you dialed
but a recorded voice greets you
informing you
that you've been automatically placed on hold

at first you can distinctly decipher
the pulsating sound of the hold button

assurance that eventually
someone will assist you
but suddenly
it's no longer audible
should you wait?
were you accidentally disconnected?
if you hang up and dial again,
will this delay their servicing your call?
so you wait
and wait
no answer
and wait

depleted of patience you slam the receiver
quickly you perform a few stress release exercises
your cool restored
you pick up the receiver
and punch the seven-note melody
by ear

You have reached Southwest Airlines.
the same recorded voice greets you anew
with modulated enthusiasm
Your call has been automatically pl—
a sweet melodic voice interrupts
"Thank you for calling Southwest Airlines—
this is Cindy, may I help you?"
"Yes, please. I need to make some reser—"
"I'm sorry . . .
but our terminals are down.
Would you like to call us back later?"
"Well, I need to catch a flight this evening."
"Well, I could take down the information, if you'd like.
But I won't be able to tell you what flights are available,
nor confirm your reservations at this time."

"I'll call back,"
you concede.
"Okay, sir.
Thank you for calling Southwest Airlines."
"Thank you."
"Bye-bye, now.
Have a nice day!"

iv.

you were assured that it would be ready by noon
punch the digits
"Hold, please."
then soon you are informed
that Mrs. Spangle is away from her desk
she's at the auditor's office picking up checks
she will return in fifteen minutes

so you wait
not fifteen
but thirty minutes
to make sure

punch the musical tones
"Hello . . .
yes, this is Mrs. Spangle . . .
I'm sorry, but the system has been down all week
and we have been unable to process payments."

there is nothing so final.

v.

is it that magic hour yet?
that sets off the daily exodus of office workers
pouring out of office buildings
cutting hurriedly across parking lots
then zipping out of downtown
in their space-age compact cars
fast as lights permit
never a minute too early
for the computer monitors
provides an accurate printout for the auditor
and gross pay can be adjusted

but once clocked out
you're on your own time
happy hour!
imperative on a Friday a minute past five

TGIF!
but you'll need some cash
that being no problem
for you've got an MPACT card
get-cash-quick facilitator
just drive on up
wait your turn, of course
then insert the card
code in the transaction
enter amount in multiples of ten
press ENTER
all systems go
and presto!
instant ca—
PLEASE REENTER TRANSACTION
it's not working
TRANSACTION INVALID
what's wrong?
now, *wait* a minute!
what?
you've got to be kidding!
it swallowed it up!
#&@!$

vi.

what the heck!
you've got some plastic
on to happy hour without further delay!
two for one!
hors d'oeuvres!
live music!
sophisticated company!

just don't end up
at one of those modern establishments
like those two tourists from San Antonio
who after hiking all day long
to the sites in San Francisco
culminated their tour
at a pub along Fisherman's Wharf

"Two cold Miller Lites!"
they happily order
"I'm sorry, sirs,"
the bartender politely responds
"but I cannot serve you
until the computer signs on."
"What?"
"¿Qué dice?"
"What do you mean, bro'?
The sign right there says
'happy hour four to seven.' "
"Yes, sir, but it's not quite four.
That clock is ahead."
and the two thristy tourists
look at each other
in disbelief
it simply does not compute.

rituals

weary-eyed, but with a ready smile
and a sweet, "Hello,
how a' you doing?"
"Fine, thank you!
An' how a' you?"
with their wigs patted on, just right
for style and for warmth
they used to ride the bus to River Oaks every a.m.
now they walk, retired
carrying those straw bags
the "missus" so graciously bequeathed them
and with makeup and talcum on their faces
and lipstick, purple red or burgundy
from those gold-plated caps
bought from Bonita
who sold Avon, door to door, years ago
luscious, just-the-right-shade lipstick
"tha's moist and stays on yo' lips"
even after a kiss
"Not like that cheap stuff
they sells at Walgreen's nowdays—
and ex*pen*sive!
Oooh, Lo'd, is things ex*pen*sive these days!"

church hat
with a veil and a rhinestone broche
a sixties three-piece outfit
impeccably pressed
thoughtfully matched
with square-heeled white leather shoes
and support hose
to aid the zig-zag walking
through the maze of massive monoliths
"Why, hello, Bev'ly! How you doing?"
"Oh, I'm good! Just catchin' me some of dis nice sun."
"Ain't it perty!"
"Mmm-hhmm, sho is."
"You looking real good."
"Why, thank you. You looking perty good yo'self."

"Oh, Lo'd, he'ah come the Shoppe'!
I see you!"
"I see you!
Says hello to yo aunt for me!"

dime clicks into money box
aged hands tuck flowered brocade coin purse
into sweater pocket
one finger is jeweled
with an antique silver wedding ring
on another is a mother's ring
counting in gems
the births of children

on the Shopper's Special
weary feet rest from where they've been
geometric right-angled approaches
like advancing points on a computer grid
to Foley's
"They having a big sale."
to Woolworth's
"Don't let me forget my Jergens."
then to the Post Office
"Gots to mail in those forms to Social Security."
then over to the County Courts cafeteria
"Yes, mam . . . I'll have me
one of them pieces of pecan pie
and coffee, please."
familiar places frequented for years
now surrounded and transformed by sky-reaching towers
"I cuts through that Allright Parking
on my way to McCory's.
Saves me lots of walking."

from the vantage point of bus windows
elders witness teenage girls
walking down Main Street
in their Calvin Klein jeans, bodytight
        "Oooh, girl! What's yo' name?"
        "Oooh, girl! Can I walk wichu!"
waiting at DON'T WALK signs
keeping time to stereophonic Motown

radio balanced on one arm
one hand left free
for gesturing and finger snapping
and singing along

> "Don't touch that ste-re-o,
> Don't touch that ste-re-o!
> Come on!
> Don't touch that ste-re-o,
> Don't touch that ste-re-o!"

pausing, for timely whisperings
into each other's ears
"Those dudes think they bad."
and breaking out in splendid laughter
that bows them to the ground
paying not much mind
to their admirers
nor to old timers standing next to them
leaning on canes, clad in fifties jackets and caps
nor to office workers behind them
tapping their feet out of synch with the music
nor noticing elders
pensively peering through tinted-glass bus windows
gazing at them
with mothers' eyes

telephone line

post-noontime customers stand in line
their umbrellas dripping
their shoes drenched
for the moment sheltered from the torrential storm
cold gusts of which
splatter sheets of rain
against the smoked-glass walls

behind the counter a young Black girl
waits on customers
chewing gum
she hands a man a yellow slip
he hurriedly walks across the room
to the customer service window
while a pair of Mexicanos
at the head of the line
for a second, hesitate
then advance from the WAIT HERE marker on the floor
to the counter
they are short and small
they wear boyish half-smiles

"What color, style and length of cord would chu like?"
the girl asks in monotone,
gazing into the distance,
popping her gum
"¿Qué?" they respond, in unison
facing each other
their short-haired heads and skinny necks
resembling the shape of question marks
"What color do you want—
blue, red, yellow, green, white, black?"
she repeats, disinterestedly
pointing to the different models
and rolling her eyes
they begin to comprehend
and pause to consider the question
quietly exchanging opinions in Spanish
gesturing with their hands

while assorted pairs of legs
shift their weight
from left foot to right foot
from right foot to left foot
one customer side steps out of line
to check and see
"What's taking so damn long?!"
some tap their feet impatiently
to the count of seconds expiring
on the wall clock
a woman standing last in line
decides to leave
while the two Mexicanos
make up their minds
several times
as to what color, style and length of cord
they would like

most likely they live in an apartment house
along with other undocumented workers
most likely the color and the style of phone
little matters to the habitat's decor
although important is
the length of cord

> "¡Ah, qué vida en los Estados Unidos!
> ¡Una tierra de pura ventaja!"

no more waiting in line at the Stop-n-Go pay phones
no more quarters lost
no more standing for hours by the Seven-Eleven phone boothes
wating on that call
from San Francisco del Rincón

> "¡Ah, qué la Juana!
> Me prometió que me llamaba a las meras tres, ¡hombre!
> Ya son después de las cinco.
> Bueno pues, vámonos ya.
> ¡Ni modo!"

wearing wide smiles on their faces
they exit out the door

walking off into the storm
in rapid strides
with no umbrellas
but with boxed telephone and directories
securely held under their arms
yes, indeed!
why, if they all chip in for the monthly bill
it's very much worth it!
what a bargain from Ma Bell!

"Créemelo—
¡Sí, costea!
¡Sí, costea!"

down on Main Street

Black hand crumples celophane candy wrapper
into a ball
one knee is casually raised up slightly
leg is moved over to one side
Black hand pushes crumpled paper
through self-closing trash receptacle
leg is casually moved back
it dangles
as she continues to sit
on top
of the trash receptacle
her posture relaxed
one arm held loosely around
the waist of a toddler
seated by her side
his wide dull eyes blinking blankly
at passing buses and cars
she, taking slow drags from a cigarette just lit
through thin lips painted frosted pink
her palid freckled face expressionless
mascaraed blue-gray eyes
fixed in a distant gaze
legs swinging slightly
sandled feet dangling
directing the viewers vision
to stenciled letters
KEEP HOUSTON CLEAN

the gospel singers

it was high noon
under bright gray skies
on a balmy day
in the center of August
when they came
opened their souls
and sang
soothing spirituals
  "Lo'd, this time
  Ah said, this time
  I'm go-ing
  all
  the way . . ."
faith in a song
crescendoing
bouncing off walls
echoing from four directions

and space
weather
sounds
became one
and pedestrians slowly gathered 'round
and listened
pensively nodding
to the rhythm
some humming along

even the bums
one by one
gathered in the plaza
and sat, placidly
in groupings
their glazed blank eyes
gazing down
or far away
while the music seeped

through long-empty spirits

somewhere deep down inside
a forgotten feeling
may have stirred?

time bomb: from an office window

about,
a brownish haze of pollution
that hugs the resplendent city skyline
superstructures
posing for eternity
their sharp shadows casting the time of day
advancing in diminishing angles
as undiscernibly
as the hour hand
of a ticking clock
finite,
irreversible

above,
nebulous skies
glory's aura
threshold to the afterlife
where some wish to go
when there's no longer future

below,
downtowners, minute
about their daily business
their arrival
at the next momentary stop
electronically monitored:
yellow
red
green
WALK
DON'T WALK
yellow
red
green

in between,
the vision of the future
glass monoliths

reflecting geometric orderliness
multitudes of Meisian eyes
gazing out of corporate cubicles
thresholds to success

and within,
the human soul
that for an instant stirs
hard-pressed to conceive
the immensity of the universe
an infinity
beyond comprehension

daily progress

inner city junior high school youths
gather at the stop
some hold books
others, ghetto blasters
their lean bodies
emanate rhythm

a dude strolls by
at an uncertain gait
he wears a pastel green shower cap
over his 'fro
intermittently he snaps his finger
looks about and over his shoulder
then steps up his pace

six old timers
sit on the steps
of a dilapidated porch
waiting for "they rides to woik"
still as in a photograph
barely visible in the dark morning shadows
of trees and shrubs
they watch the 8 a.m. traffic zoom by
"shootin' de breeze"
discussing last night's poker game
making plans for the evening
plotting subsistence
a way out of the day
into tomorrow

an elderly woman stands
waiting for the bus
she leans slightly on a cane
a flowered silk scarf
contains her features
alert eyes
high cheekbones
smooth dark skin
fine wrinkles

behind her stands
the white-washed structure of a baptist church
bare and erect
its steeple pointing
the way

across the street
two tall, lanky boys
walk in synchronized strides
nudging each other
talking, laughing loudly
waving their arms in sporadic gestures
each carries a varsity gym bag

down the street
rows of shanties
shotgun houses
leaning in odd directions
ramshackled by shifting foundations;
layers of paint, brittle and chipped
exposed wood
a weathered ashen gray brown
as in the hue of skin
of the aged hands of a white-haired woman
in a pastel blue housedress
tending to her roses
humming a spiritual
"Mmmmmmhhhhh-mmmhhhhmmmmmhh . . ."
sprinkling water
from a Folger's coffee can
on the thirsty thorny-stemmed bushes

an old, battered station wagon
approaches the day
its rectangular-shaped rear window
framing the silhouettes
of five middle-aged men
their stout bodies crowded together
each gazing in distinct directions
at red lights one man in the back seat
leans forward to talk to the driver

who responds with words and gestures
and the tapping of ashes off his cigarette
out the window onto the street
his eyes remain fixed
on the traffic ahead
when the light turns green
the station wagon floats over bumps and dips
like a boat over waves of water
off to the toils
of a Tuesday

"KTSU-U-U-you-you . . ."
echoes the sexy stereophonic voice
of a female disc jockey
on cue
her sibilants distinct
". . . We are effective,
efficient
and provocative!"
the whispering voice projects
in digital delay
fading into
percussive expansive rhythms
which permeate the Ward
in the measures of calypso
"Oh-oh, yeah!
We're gonna have a party!
All night lo-ng! All night!"
Lionel Richie promises
a group of children
prance and skip
across the school yard
in the distance
in perfect timing to the music
they cannot hear

down the block
a lonely figure sits on a stool
in the tiny porch of a small frame house
his hands rest idly on his lap
he watches the parade of people
in cars

city trucks
buses and bicycles
on foot
all in a hurry
his eyes, now blurred of vision
have seen more than most
he has lived here all his life
the "Wa'd" is as it's always been
"Save a few Spanish folks
an' Vietnamese
dats moved into de neighb'hd
he-ah an' the-ah . . ."

a car idles at the stoplight
its muffler rumbles loudly
Motown resounds
the driver turns the volume down
he leans out the window
grinning widely
at a big-boned girl walking by
"Say! Say, girl!
What's yo' name?
I be talkin' to you, in the red!"
at the DON'T WALK sign, she stops
nonchalantly she turns to look at him
"What chu want, fool?"
"Shoot! What chu mean,
'What chu want, fool?'
Shoot! You gonna be dat way,
I won' even look a' chu!"
the light turns green
and the smart dude speeds off
in his blue Impala
burning rubber
feigning triumph

on the next street
at a park corner
an evangelist hails
a bible in one hand
a small megaphone in the other
he preaches to passing motorists

"Repent!
Repent and see the light!
And walk that golden path to Salvation!"
when there are no motorists or pedestrians
he directs his sermon
seemingly to the trees and heavens
and doesn't hesitate to kick away
a stray pup
that meekly tries to huddle at his side

the next street block is bustling
with office workers scurrying into buildings
beauties in high fashions
kiss their husbands or lovers
a morning good-bye
with poise they step out of expensive cars
in smart high heels they strutt off with their stuff
vanishing into the corridors of AT&T
but not before
men's eyes check out
their merchandise and others'
as long as it remains in view
while motorists in the lanes behind them
honk their horns impatiently
"Move it!
Move it on, buddy!"

at the street adjacent
little old white ladies
in fifties faded pastel sweaters
and translucent nylon scarves
wait on buses
nervous as birds
apprehension painted on their faces
they stand alongside
middle-aged working women
with patience in their eyes
they've seen much
"Mmm-huhh! Yes, indeed!"
their hefty arms crossed at their chests
"I gots all the time."

some wear white starched uniforms
some carry department store shopping bags
"You best not mess wit' me!"
one glares at a street bum
not to be trusted
in line behind her
and she clutches her purse tighter
as she boards the bus

down the street
clusters of Black and Hispanic teenagers
approach with reluctance
their threshold to alternative success
Contemporary Educational Training Center
two Latin teenage girls linger behind
sacrificing tardy marks
hurriedly they share
the last drags of a cigarette
it's cool to smoke
affirms the provocative pose
of an All-American handsome
on the billboard, overhead

meanwhile, at the next street corner
handsome teenagers await buses
en route to a distinct destiny
in designer clothes, they pose
like models in a catalogue
some have music cases at their side
others, stacks of books
to the High School for the Visual and Performing Arts
they're bound
in their minds
the echo of advice
"You best study ha'd.
Don't be a fool, son.
I've woiked ha'd fo' you to git
the opp'tunity we didn' git.
You make somethin' of yo'self, son . . .
Make yo' Momma
and yo' Daddy
proud."

dumb broad!

dumb broad!
I'm believing it 'cause I'm seeing it!
dumb broad!
keep your eyes on the road, stupid!
a man sits next to her, motionless
oblivious
why don't you comb your hair at home, you stupid broad!
I mean, I've seen women yank off their steam rollers
at stop lights
then brandish brush
and drive, one-handed
while expertly arranging their hair
with a few, quick precision strokes
at times you must
to get to work on time
but, oh!
I cannot believe this!
look!
now she is teasing her hair!
stupid broad!
I'd hate to be in the car ahead of her
she can't see the traffic behind her
for she's got the rearview mirror in a perpendicular position
while she touches up her eye makeup
at first with quick casual glances
but now, very intently peering into hazard
I mean, I know one gets distracted
you look into the mirror to touch up your lipstick
and you end up re-doing your eyeshadow
heavens, you knew you should've worn hyacinth
instead of celery
it looks so different in the daylight!

look at her!
I can't believe she's teasing her hair!
and with both hands off the steering wheel
and in fast-moving, bumper-to-bumper 8 a.m. traffic
at a five-point intersection
and a school zone at that!

and the passive passenger sits!
doesn't budge!
could he be her husband who's simply given up on her,
his nagging was of no use?
or, perhaps he's just a car pooler
with no choice in the matter
or simply unaware
that his life is in danger!

now, *wait* a minute!
I'm believing this as I'm seeing it!
she is now spraying her hair generously
in round, swooping motions
utilizing both the rearview and sideview mirrors
which she has expertly adjusted for this purpose
the traffic is of no concern to her
and the passenger remains a mannequin
except for one slow-motion glance
over at her and back
as she squirts the mist
on her mass of teased hair
and on his bald head

we have advanced four blocks
there she drives ahead of me
sporting a splendid hair-do
she brakes on and off, sporadically
as she shifts her weight around in her seat
finding a position of comfort
while tuning the radio
once settled, she flicks her bic
at a cigarette that's stuck in her mouth
she looks over
puffs smoke at the face of the motionless passenger
who obligingly hands her
a cup of steaming coffee

dumb broad!

order and law

weekday mornings
exodus of humanity
convergence
at the criminal courts building
where the aftermath of crime lingers
people crowding into elevators
waiting in the hallways
entering courtrooms
taking their places
the hour arrives
the judicial process ensues
the record begins
oaths are administered
pleas are entered
the jury is seated
and actors live their roles
putting forth their best speech
explanations
alibis
yes-no answers
emphatic whisperings at the bench
while curious spectators,
their faces expectant,
await the sound of the gavel:

justice rules
with severe finality
one defendant cries
another smiles at his luck
one victim is avenged
another's plea is misconstrued

justice is final

space

privacy that no one owns
a silent moment
outdoors, in the city
the shade of a tree at a park
a vacant table at a library
your own office window with your own view
beaches and sea
body-free
your own breath of air
an expansive horizon
viewed by many
but singularly

C^3I: news flash

the times are not conducive
to pondering aesthetics
the muse is not just
predictably elusive
it is absent
withdrawn to its nebulous origins
it does not belong
in a state of alert
that clear possibility
menacing
invading our repose
the dinner hour
when we gulp our morsels
at the edge of our seats
witnessing on the screen
riots
bombings
massacres
in bleeding colors
history documented before our eyes
via satellite
analyzed
editorialized
scripted
edited
up-dates
bulletins
briefs
interrupting our favorite sit-coms:

we pray that the news
never arrives
one second
too late

the bridge people

against the futuristic buildings
and hustle and bustle of downtown
the winos, the bums
the downtrodden
hold their ground
their niche secure
in a scheme of existence
based on time that must advance
all meet a precise fate
the weak, the strong
the damned, the blessed
the wretched, the fortunate
the shrewd, the innocent
beings of distinct destinies
co-existing, side by side

precarious is the balance

metropolis: time of the season

When the rain comes
They run and hide their heads
They might as well be dead . . .
—from "Rain" by John Lennon and
Paul McCartney

it is the first storm
of the hurricane season
the rain falls horizontally
now vertically
now at criss-cross angles
suddenly—
a scatter of hail
spear-like droplets
descending forcefully
intermittently becoming
a soft, delicate sprinkle

the sky that minutes ago
turned dark as night
now glows an opaque silverwhite
clouds rush by
in thin layers
Old Glory, that daily hails
from the dome of the courthouse
someone quickly took down

in the downtown square
the limbs of trees sway and bend
to erratic tropical gusts
about, downtowners escape from the rain
scurrying into buildings
some carrying umbrellas
others holding newspapers over their heads
while by the gurgling fountain
on a park bench
sits a bum
drenched by the downpour
calling toasts

drinking nothing
from an empty soda water bottle
and waving and smiling
at imaginary passers-by

fish are jumping

a mirror of fluid tranquility
lies captive in the bay
in the quiet of morning
the seagulls and the pelicans
begin to awaken
their calls, occasional

in the canal
the intermittent sounds
like those of pebbles splashing into a pond
ripples expanding outwardly
in circular patterns
gradually vanishing
marking the path
of mullets, swimming in line
one behind the other
leaping out in sequence
gasping
then dipping back into
the green waters
with a soft, quiet splash
plip! out
and splash! back in
a jump-and-a-gasp
for life
sustenance

about, a halo of fog
magically dissipates
revealing distant lights
twinkling indigo
and yellow-orange
the silhouettes of refineries
in the horizon
across the bay

and, slowly
that vision blurs
as the photographer adjusts the lens

sharpening the focus
on mullets, swimming in line
one behind the other
from their spawning areas bound for the depths
plip! jump! gasp-for-breath! down, splash!
plip! jump! gasp-for-life! splash!
plip! jump! gasp! splash!
and disappear
into the undercurrent-ridden waters
treacherous below
that illusory surface
of cool, green tranquility

many great fishermen have waded in these emerald waters
their fates crossing those of schools of fish
in a moment of truth
some have whispered
an urgent prayer

fishermen peer

retired fishermen
casting their lines off the San Francisco Bay
"We're all retired Navy,
all the fishermen you see here,"
the old one uttered
motioning towards still figures
poised with rods and reels

"Ouch!"
he punctured his finger
with the hook
"I always do this,
every time I start talking to someone!"

retired fishermen
silent profiles confessing their solitude to the sea
". . . all retired Navy"
as in the faded, wrinkled navy-blue pants that they wear
as in their life-laden postures
as in the resolute expressions on their faces
Irish, Mexican,
German, Italian,
Philippino
unlikely elements, united
as countrymen
facing a war-torn destiny
now their past

San Francisco Bay fisherman's pier
here the trails of time and toil converge
and at once spark that pulse
the mingling of souls
the birth of a gifted giant
its many faces reflected in the aquamarine mirror
a sea of downward glances
slanted eyes, deep-blue eyes
almond-brown eyes, eagle-black eyes
intense eyes
sad eyes

content eyes
gazing into the depths of heaven
peering through that waterglass window of eternity
meeting fate
face to face

encanto

never have you heard this song
yet you've always known it
rhythm as constant
as the waves of the ocean
against the giving sand

never have you heard this song
yet you've always known it
emotions evoked
by the magic
of a silverblue full moon:

taunting melody
arriving from the depths of the singer's soul
words sensuous as kisses
enticing you to taste them
claim the pleasure
you have always sought

never have you heard this song
yet therein it dwells
deep in your imagination
like an enchanted memory
tugging at your soul:

the vocalist confesses
in the honest words of a song
your mind conceives
and your heart rings
enraptured

progress

the foreman keeps a general watch
while the operator works his muscle and skill
at crank and pulley
aiming expertly
13,000 pounds of steel
smashing windows first
boom!
glass shattering
cascading down like water and broken sheets of ice
along with ornamental ironworks
boom!
fractured, gray chunks of cement
toppling down
in slow motion
revealing redbrick walls
boom!
sunlight seeping through the haze
of pulverized ashen plaster
exposing dingy interior walls
the colors of the plastic sixties
dim yellow, lime greens and aquablues:
whose souls did these walls harbor?
what thoughts went mixed in the plaster?
whose weathered hands stacked the brick, one by one?
what hopes, once molded and sealed in mortar,
lie shattered, exposed?
what modern mysteries lie, cracked open?

and the operator works methodically
aiming at consistent intervals
blow upon blow
at the walls
boom!
then at the mounds of rubble
iron piers and rusted pipes
imbedded, under brick and cement
boom!
smashing it
boom!

mashing it
with expert skill
motor roaring
shifts and gears

precariously, the wrecking ball rises
a pendulum gaining momentum
laden with power
it hovers high over the hollowed edifice
readying for a strategic plunge
boom!
it misses its aim
toppling down the side of a wall
onto the rubble
slowly, the "headache" ball rises
while the foreman, eyes alert
watches the progress
and the surrounding traffic
of motor vehicles and pedestrians
business as usual
save a few downtowners, who hasten their strides
covering their faces
escaping from the dust
while window washers
balanced on scaffolds at the building adjacent
squint their eyes and frown
as dust veils their faces
and the windows they just washed
intently they witness
the final giving of the structure
13,000 pounds of steel descending
BOOM!
crashing squarely on the rooftop
it caves in with an explosion
a massive cloud of dust rises high
and spreads across a five-block radius

gradually the dust settles
unveiling the new horizon
Main Street and its anachronistic landmarks
the backdrop, opaque glass towers
modern versions of the gothic

time's continuum
sculptured

the decades-old building is gone
its shadow vanished to the ground
its burial site

disfiguring in the process of genesis
notes the intellect;
incessantly destroying the old, incessantly creating the new
states the industrialist;
inconoclastic invention
contends the artist

yet, "What's wrong with copying?"
the architect flatly challenges
construing that a vital premise
has been "wrong,
simply wrong."

they're everywhere

you can see them
gathered around ice-chests
guzzling the day's refreshing rewards
they are of all breeds
northerners relocated south
hippy types, their blond hair pulled back in ponytails
and with tatoos on their arms
Blacks, native and transient
young and old
rednecks, from neighboring rural towns
chucos, with their bandanas,
baggy pants, white undershirts
"illegals," with their disheveled hair
puzzled looks
stooped postures
you can see them everywhere
standing alongside street curbs
their sixpacks on the fenders of dilapidated cars
you can see them, unscheming
youths intermingling with men
drinking down the toil of the day
the cool, intoxicating liquid refreshes
soothes weary muscles
brings drunken detachment
from the monetary demands of every day
heavy as steel and concrete
you can see them
standing outside apartment buildings
or seated on the steps of duplex porches
or hanging out at convenience stores
or huddled around car repair garages
looking like the greasers that they're called
wearing drunken smiles

you can see them during the day
in utility trucks
loaded along with tools and equipment
among the junk and debri they've collected
and one day you may chance to notice him

seated on the bed of a pick-up
amid a group of youths
at the wheel, a red-faced Anglo
gearing lives
you may note his mature visage
his staunch posture
his grayed hair
contrasting with the others' heads of black
and through the window of your car
for a finite instant
your eyes may meet
he'll quickly look away
you'll quickly look away
intuition tells you to
and his gaze remains fixed
on the road ahead
although he is aware of you
as he is of the Cadillac
that tailgates the pick-up
its ruddy-faced driver slouched in his seat
puffing on a cigar
his forehead wrinkled in a frown
he steps on it
and passes up the truck
not having distinguished
the elder among youths
that man among boys
all equal
whose glance may have once crossed yours
at destiny's intersection

you can see them after work
when it's happy hour
at convenience stores
that bank on their salaries
you can see them after five
at street corners
or in the parking lots
of bars and ice-houses

"This neighborhood didn't used to be this way,"
the eldest resident on the block declares
you can see them everywhere

threshold: toys or us

automatic double doors open:

"You carry the box,
I'll carry the baby."
"I'd rather carry the baby—
he's lighter. *You* carry the box."
"Fine—
"—at least this one doesn't move around!"
"This one hugs!"

automatic double doors shut.

what a *#&(!

as the bus approached
three young women and a middle-aged Black man
stepped forward
from where they had waited
among others
by the jewelry store
by the bake shop
by the loan agency
casually they had gathered around the Metro Stop
readying transfers and coins
rearranging purses and bags
but the bus sped past them
halting abruptly at the corner street light
breaks screeching piercingly loud
hydraulic-powered doors
slamming noisily ajar

and they ran to the corner
squinting at the trail of heat and exhaust
and the whirlwind of particles and dust
stirred up by the bus
"I don't believe she felt like stopping for us,"
one of the women said to the man
as they started to board
"Tha's a lady fo' you,"
he uttered
shaking his head
"Would it a-been a man drive'
he wouldn' a done dat.
Tha's a lady fo' you."

patience

cast the silverspoon
toss it with a wish
like a penniful of thoughts
into a good luck pond

cast the silverspoon
out it reels with a hum
its path a graceful arch
that cuts across an orange sunburst
meeting morning skies
and waking waters
in symmetry

cast the silverspoon
toss it in with a prayer
as many times as faith permits
then reel it in
with a harmonic hum:

the ocean is spilling with treasures
for those who look deep

full-page

jot it down
hurry!
deadlines ensue
don't bother just yet
to punctuate
the hour hand advances
when you're not looking
the second hand alarms
with its conspicuous rapidity
IF YOU DON'T KEEP UP,
YOU'LL BE LEFT BEHIND.
the ad adverts

city cemetery

and all have gone home now
to rest
have walked away
advancing across the expanse of blue and green
heads bowed
eyes downcast
veils heavy
tears blurring vision
each footstep a weight
sinking into soft dewy grass
gravity pulling
wanting more:

only the fragrance lingers
fresh flowers withering in the noon sun
shrouding the mound
of moist, black earth
bright yellows, reds and whites
singing out
defying sadness

a quiet moment

distant groans
of steel machinery
originating from industrial yards
by night

faraway barks
of neighborhood dogs
echoing
in chain reaction

the thundering propellers
of a police helicopter
hovering
floodlights scanning rooftops
backyards
streets

the audible motor presence
of the freeway
an aura of inertia
eighteen wheelers breaking limits
sirens
growing louder
fading

muffled bass notes
of a guitar
emanating from next door
penetrating layers of walls

silence . . .
the sudden hush of night breezes
percussive
limbs of trees stirring
leaves fluttering
inciting the cricket
into a summer song

elusive symphonics

the wind-carried cadence
of a marching band
at a stadium close by

the hard slam of a car door
engine igniting
car tearing off
into the darkened depths
of residential streets
muffler roaring
first gear . . .
second . . .
third

drip-drop
the persistent
drip-drip drop
of a leaking faucet

squeak
the squeak and tinkle
of ice
as it melts
cracks
in a sweating glass of water

ri-ng!
the faint, urgent
ri-ng!
a call that on one answers

thu-thump . . thu-thump . .
heartbeat
pulsating in your ear
your mind resting
on a pillow of twilight dreams

sudden wakefulness:
the lonely bellow
of a foghorn
embracing the night
a foreign ship

exiting the Port

rap-rap-rap!
a sudden, barely discernible
rap-rap-rap-rap-rap!
conscience knocking
at your door

aims at you between the eyes

The case is perfect against you, all the documents say so—in spite of the fact that it is reasonably certain that you were not at the scene of the crime . . .

from "Impromptu: The Suckers"
by William Carlos Williams

the true enemy
is all around
as sure are those invisible contaminants
emitted day and night
by twentieth century timebombs
for the lungs of future generations
but that's just domestic violence
industrial, technological pursuit
in the name of science
that carries big accounts
who would not *want* to
be involved?

but what is being thought of
is the true enemy
that assaults
in the first degree
at airports
in high security conference rooms
in battle zones
and in remote villages
of unrecognized sovereign nations
but that's only foreign violence
undeclared and unofficial
and everyone knows who the participating forces are
and what they want
for people read the paper
and they watch the news
and they remember
and figure it out for themselves

given, with the help of subliminal marketing
the genius of salesmanship
that seduces
slices the butter
makes nothing sacred
and truths universal

but what is being thought of
is the true enemy
through psychokinesis
a faithful companion
at home you power it onto the screen
by reflex reaction:
astute editorialism
pronounced in predictable patterns
of inflection
pause
monotone
flashing images
of modern day miracles
miseries
scientific breakthroughs
setbacks
explosive scenes
shocking tragedies
which you can compute or reject
by remote control

ensconsed in the comfort of an easy chair
a haven of retreat is the home
where feelings of security surge
you and yours are safe
but who is not?
the headlines will tell
of likely and unlikely victims
Darwinian theory affirmed
the world as it's always been
wherein laws
can instantly become nonfunctional
like a computer, down
a bankrupt bank of objective intelligence
deeming imperative

emergency backup
the human factor
the output
not always reliable
someone will have to pay the price
another diffused old truth
and a premise at once
uncompelling and complex
too common for most
a challenge
only for a genius posed

ARTE
PUBLICO
PRESS

0 00 02 0462863 0
MIDDLEBURY COLLEGE

Evangelina Vigil-Piñón

The Computer Is Down is at once a celebration of the crystalline an silvery image of the modern city, its advanced technology and economi power, as well as an iconoclastic questioning of the values attendant to thi late twentieth century monument of civilization. The poet's eye guides th reader beyond the blinding glitter and the dizzying pace of the "spac city" to focus on street and neighborhood life, on the common man in hi adaptation—happy or uneasy—to what seems to be an increasingly dehu manizing urban environment.

In *The Computer Is Down*, our Virgil leads us down into the bowels of th city, where inhabit the human detritus: the downtrodden, the ignored, th forgotten. And above, at street level, the beauty of people maintainin their culture and traditions, unknowingly resisting dehumanization, re sounds above the din of the traffic, the air drill and the wrecking ball Like the black teens swaggering up the block to their "ghetto blaster" radios and the retired "rich folks' " maids steadily marching to an inter nal, more profound beat, the common folk shall endure—longer than th towers of Ozymandias.

Evangelina Vigil-Piñón is a Fellow of the National Endowment for th Arts and winner of numerous literary awards, including First Place in national contest sponsored by the Coordinating Council of Literary Maga zines. Ms. Vigil-Piñón has been widely published in literary magazine throughout the country and is the author of a chapbook, *Nade y Nad* (1978), a first collection of poems, *Thirty an' Seen a Lot* (1982) and a anthology, *Woman of Her Word: Hispanic Women Write* (1983). The Sa Antonio native currently resides in Houston, where she works for *Th Americas Review* as an editor.

Cover Art and Design: Mark A. Piñón

Arte Publico Press
University of Houston
Houston, Texas 77004

ISBN 0-934770-32-8
LC 83-072576